Dragon Eggs Book 4

Dragon's Fire

Emily Martha Sorensen

Also by Emily Martha Sorensen

Standalones:
Black Magic Academy

Fairy Senses:
Fairy Eyeglasses
Fairy Compass
Fairy Earmuffs
Fairy Barometer
Fairy Pox
Fairy Slippers
Fairy Lunchbox
Fairy Icepack

Dragon Eggs:
Dragon's Egg
Dragon's Hope
Dragon's First Christmas

Comics:
A Magical Roommate
To Prevent World Peace

The End in the Beginning:
The Keeper and the Rulership
The Fires of the Rulership
The Magic or the Rulership

Trilogy of a Teenage Werevulture:
Trials of a Teenage Werevulture

The Numbers Just Keep
Getting Bigger:
Twenty-Four Potential
Children of Prophecy

Magical Mayhem:
To Prevent World Peace
To Prevent Chic Costumes

Short Story Collections:
Worlds of Wonder

Picture Books:
Tabby, Tabby, Burning Bright

Dragon Eggs Book #4: Dragon's Fire
Copyright © 2017 by Emily Martha Sorensen
Cover art by Eva Urbaníková

All rights reserved. Printed in the United States of America.

ISBN-13: 978-1-949607-05-5
ISBN-10: 1-949607-05-4

http://www.emilymarthasorensen.com

To Liz,

who has done a lot of urgent,
last-minute beta-reading for me,
even when it was personally inconvenient.

Thank you for that.

Thank you also for that whole
"being a great sister" thing.
That makes it really nice to be around you.

Chapter 1
Forward

The zoo was filled with people and an air of festivity. It was the third day of the New Year, the crowd was brimming with excitement for the future, and a tiny blue dragon infant was sharing one of her mother's memories.

She was a beautiful, vain dragon, vibrantly blue, stretching out her long neck to show off her horns to the prospective mate she wished to have notice her. The purple male ignored her, so she snorted fire in exasperation. Must he be clueless? She had been hoping to be coy.

She raised her wings in a sharp flapping motion. That caught the male's attention for a moment, so she kept on beating them steadily, as if to launch off the ground.

Of course she knew that she could no longer fly. She was too heavy. Flight was something only the smallest dragons kept to adulthood. In fact, loss of flight was usually seen as a sign of maturity and readiness to procreate.

Still, as with most dragons who reached adulthood, she could still glide. She climbed atop the pile of boulders she had prepared, waiting until she was sure the male was watching. Spreading her wings widely, she launched herself downwards, floated for a moment as the air caught her momentum, and then floated with easy grace to the ground.

Yes. Now she had his attention. She flapped her wings and moved close enough to catch it as he let escape a flash of memory of how beautiful she'd been on her glide down.

She fluttered her wings and waited for the admiration to continue. She coyly kept her memories to herself as she admired the vibrant red-purple of his scales, different enough from her own color to show that he was not closely related, and therefore eligible.

Oh, come now! He was walking away! Well, fine then! She would be much more aggressive!

Rose drew in a deep breath as she came back to herself. The window into the courtship behaviors of another species was fascinating, and it was no wonder that the crowd seemed so enthralled, pushing closer and shouting for more.

Still, Rose thought. *Still . . .*

Violet was very pleased that they liked her mother's memory! Violet would share one of her father's!

No, Rose thought. *You're more than just a repository of your ancestors' experiences. You're a very small child. You should be . . .*

A new memory washed over her.

His second child was poking at the new egg. The purple boy wanted to know when his sister would hatch.

Not yet, he indicated to the curious boy. And poking the egg with one's claws was not a good thing. The little baby would be inside the egg for another season. Until then . . .

Tears sprang to Rose's eyes as the memory faded, and she pushed backwards to get away. She pushed through the crowd until she was reasonably sure the small blue dragon could not pick up her thoughts, and then she leaned against the bars of a cage with her head in her hands.

All dead. They're all dead. Every one of those people in her memories is dead.

It was obvious, and yet nobody here seemed to realize the implications. Dragons had gone extinct hundreds of thousands of years ago, all save the few *Deinonychus antirrhopus* eggs that had miraculously been recovered recently.

Chapter 1: Forward

Rose composed herself with difficulty, breathing in deeply. Her son was the other dragon in New York City, and she must not let herself think too much about that tragedy. The last thing she or Henry or Virgil needed was for the three-month-old baby to remember just how much he had lost, and how much he could never regain.

Focus on the future, Rose reminded herself, opening her eyes. *Their species was lost, as was their entire civilization, and yet now they both have a second chance. There are now two living dragons in New York City, one in Washington D.C., and four in Vernal. Soon there might be* Deinonychus antirrhopus *all over the country.*

A smile rose on her lips at the reminder, and Rose pulled away from the empty cage. It almost did not even bother her that it was empty because it had been reserved in case a third dragon hatched in their city.

She pushed through the crowd, burying her disappointment that the crowd had been too thick to have a private conversation with her son's friend, and exited the zoo into Central Park. She strode through the partially-frozen slush across the walkways, pondering the amusing courtship of Violet's parents.

Will Virgil one day court Violet that way? Rose wondered. *Will he be clueless, and she forward? Of course, he might choose another girl altogether, given that there is already one female in Washington D.C. and another in Vernal . . .*

"Absurd, you know," a woman was saying to a companion by her side, both of them walking briskly past Rose. "How could anyone call that thing the same as human? It's an insult, that's what it is."

Rose bristled, and she quickened her pace without conscious thought to keep up with the women. Angry as it made her, she wanted to know what people were saying about her son's species. She wanted to know what attitudes she would have to overcome to get her son the acceptance he would need.

The other woman bobbed her head in agreement. She wore an admiring look that implied little capacity for thoughts of her own.

"Really," the first woman went on, waving an arm clad in a thick fur coat. Her hat was the peak of fashion, and her shining boots were either brand new or immaculately kept. "It should be obvious, shouldn't it, just by the fact that the zoo is the proper place to keep those things, that they are no more than animals?"

Rose's blood boiled.

"Very obvious," the second woman agreed.

"In fact, the very *shape* makes that clear," the first woman went on.

"Quite clear," the second woman nodded.

"Therefore, as for the parallels your husband attempted to draw between this and our own movement," the first woman sniffed, "you can see that they are quite unsubstantiated. *We* are people who deserve equal rights, whereas *those* are —"

"Excuse me," Rose broke in, unable to bear it any longer. She should, perhaps, have held her peace, but the arrogant woman had offended her last sensibility. "I beg your pardon for intruding, but you are quite wrong."

The finely-dressed woman turned around, giving Rose an arch look. A fur stole that perfectly matched her coat slid off her shoulder, and she pushed it back into place.

"I beg *your* pardon?" she asked sarcastically.

Rose's heart thundered in her chest. She was aware of the rudeness of eavesdropping, and she should no doubt have let them pass without keeping pace, but now that she had heard the woman's words, she could not let them stand.

"*Deinonychus antirrhopus* dragons have long been suspected of intelligence, and now that suspicion has been replaced with certainty," Rose said in a level voice. "Intellectually, they are our equals. Perhaps more than equals, for they have abilities our species has never gained."

The second woman looked very offended.

"Did you vote?" the woman in the fur coat demanded.

Rose blinked, taken aback. "I . . . . beg your pardon?"

"Did you *vote*?" the fur-coated woman asked insistently.

What has that to do with anything? Rose wondered.

Chapter 1: Forward

She vaguely recalled a great deal of commotion last year over the Nineteenth Amendment passing, but she had never paid that much attention to politics, and Virgil had awoken shortly after that. When the election had come in November, she had been far too busy to place any importance on whether the next president would be James Cox or Warren Harding.

Even if she had been eligible, she would not have bothered. Thankfully, she had a better answer than that.

"I was not twenty-one in November. I was not eligible." Rose brushed a strand of hair behind her ear in a businesslike manner. "But I do not see what that has to do with the subject at hand."

"Have you not read the papers?" the second woman asked angrily. "Have you not read the article today that mocked the whole cause of women's suffrage by comparing it with —"

She stopped abruptly, her hand flying to her mouth.

The woman with the fur coat sniffed and tossed her head. "If you have never fought for a cause, you cannot possibly conceive the insult implied by such an inappropriate —"

"Bessie," the second woman whispered, tugging the arm of the fur-coated woman with great urgency. "Bessie. Bessie. She was *in* the papers!"

Chapter 2
Fame

With misgiving, Rose watched the fur-coated woman's face shift from disdain to recognition.

"You're one of the so-called 'parents,'" she said with great interest. "I saw it in the papers. Your husband is a student of archeology."

"It's paleontology, and *I'm* the one who's studying it," Rose said heatedly. The papers frequently misreported that fact, and this tended to so enrage her that Henry had informed her that he would be much obliged if she would *stop* reading the papers.

"So you have a pet dragon," the second woman said.

"I have a *son* who is a dragon," Rose snapped.

"What's the difference?" the second woman asked.

Rose stared at her incredulously.

"Are you saying," the fur-coated woman asked with an odd gleam in her eye, "that a human infant is exactly the same as one of those . . . things?"

Rose recognized the gleam. She saw it often in her father's eyes when he was trying to pick a fight. She knew that it would do little good to contradict someone with that facial expression, but she could not stop herself from rising to the bait. Her son's honor was at stake.

"Not exactly the same, no. But he's equivalent."

"In what way?" the fur-coated woman asked sharply.

"He's every bit as intelligent," Rose said. "He chose us as his parents. And the meaning was clear: *parents*, nothing less. He was not even aware that we weren't dragons until he hatched."

In fact, Virgil still got mixed up over that sometimes. Just this morning, Virgil had asked her to play smack-each-other's-tail with him. She had had to remind him, for what felt like the thousandth time, that she did not have a tail.

"But the shape is far too different," the fur-coated woman said. "No one would accept a thing like that as a child."

"Henry did," Rose said. "I did. Our parents all consider him their grandson, and our neighbors accept him, as well. Once you know him, it's impossible to *not* know he's a person."

The fur-coated woman surveyed her for a long moment. "Very well," she said. "Then I'll have one, too."

Rose stared at her. "Excuse me?"

The woman reached up to adjust her hat, pulling out a long pin and sticking it back into her hair. "I'll have one, too. Francis has been saying he wants a child, and this will save me the bother of bearing one. Plus, the uniqueness will no doubt attract attention, and get us invited to the best parties."

Rose stared at her in horror. "That's an *appalling* reason to adopt a child! Not to mention that no dragon would ever choose you, with an attitude like that!"

"What Bessie wants, Bessie gets," the fur-coated woman proclaimed, waving her hand. "I'm sure these childish creatures will be no different."

Rose's mouth fell open at the sheer audacity. She was sure there could be no possible worse parent than this. Had this woman approached Virgil, he would have ignored her completely!

A sudden thought struck, making her uneasy. *What if not all the dragons will be so certain what they want? What if the certainty of someone else's mind may be enough to persuade one to make a terrible decision?*

It was true that Violet was more pliable than Virgil. She did whatever the crowd asked her, most of the time.

Surely persuasion does not become less effective just because one communicates by thoughts rather than words, Rose thought, unsettled. *Lies might be ineffective, but persuasion might be more so.*

She did not want a dragon child to wind up with this woman who would see them as a convenience, or as a trophy. But she could not think of a way to prevent it, save for hoping that all of the future dragons would more closely resemble Virgil than Violet. And that, she could not bring herself to do. She hoped that all the dragons would have unique personalities.

The second woman stared at her friend, appalled. "You would try to appease Francis with a *pet?* Really, Bessie!"

"You heard her," the fur-coated woman said, waving her hand toward Rose. "She said everyone considers them babies. Far less work for all the credit. Who wouldn't want that?"

"That is *not* what I said," Rose snapped through clenched teeth. "There is nothing about Virgil that is less work than a human infant. In fact —"

"Here is my card," the fur-coated woman said grandly, reaching into her reticule to remove a small pink card that held a large name in script in the middle, with a small address in the left corner. She held it out to Rose. "Be a dear and call upon me when one comes available, will you?"

Rose glanced down at the card, then flicked her gaze back up. She didn't take it. "I don't think you understand," she said tightly. "*Deinonychus* dragons are people. They are every bit as much work as a child you gave birth to would be."

The fur-coated woman smiled comfortably. "That's only true for poor families. When you have the means to hire a nursemaid, parenting is a breeze!"

Rose stared at her in indignation.

A snort came from the woman's companion, who sounded rather like she wished to disagree. When Rose glanced over, she saw the second woman's mouth twitching, attempting to hide an incredulous smile.

Rose's ire was slightly appeased. Perhaps the fur-coated woman's friend would be able to talk some sense into her.

Chapter 2: Fame

"I will not argue this any further," Rose said coldly. "I will only say that the desire to make one's life easier is not a wish that will be fulfilled by adopting a child. Good day."

She walked off, her heels clicking against the sidewalk and splunshing through the piles of slush that were difficult to avoid. The chill of the weather did nothing to cool the broiling state of her temper, nor the fact that she blamed herself for it.

Why did you imagine starting that discussion would be a good idea? Rose berated herself as she drove her hands into her pockets, seeking to warm them up from the chill of the air. *What could you have possibly hoped to gain?*

She knew what she had been hoping to gain. She had been hoping to educate the ignorant, to clear up an insidious wrong belief, and to stand up for the rights of her son, whether or not those women's opinions would have any bearing on his future.

Yet instead, she had given one of those women an awful idea. A life of luxury might seem appealing, and Rose was envious of any family who would never have to waste time worrying about where graduate school tuition might come from, but a child who would be raised by somebody other than his parents, a child who would be put out for display . . . how would that be any different from the zoo?

Not her, Rose thought fervently, ignoring the cold seeping through a hole in her shoe. *Not that woman. Please.*

If someone like that became able to adopt a dragon, it would undermine everything Rose had gone through, everything she was currently going through, to raise Virgil as her own. It would encourage more trophy-seekers to attempt to force their will on fragile young minds. It would be bad for the one child, bad for others who hatched later, and bad for *Deinonychus antirrhopus* in general in New York City. Perhaps across the country.

Virgil's future must be secured. The future of his species must be secured.

If only she knew how.

Rose stepped through one too many slush puddles, and noticed at last how drenched her stockings had become.

She lifted her skirt slightly, seeing that the hem was stiff with mud and water, and sighed.

It was a miserable day for walking. She wished she could have taken the bus, but their meager budget was not in agreement with consistent indulgences like that.

CHAPTER 3
Fault

"Oh, look!" Henry cried a few weeks later, reading the morning paper as he cut his breakfast omelet with the side of his fork. "There are two more eggs awake at the museum! Two at once! I'm surprised that nobody called to tell us. I mean, it's not directly our business, but it certainly is indirectly."

Rose froze in her position of frying eggs over the stove. They sizzled in the pan, the yolks starting to cook through instead of remaining runny.

"Is that so?" she asked carefully. "Does it, um . . . does it say who the parents will be?"

She had not told Henry about her encounter outside the zoo on the day she had been coming back home from Monday classes. Mostly this had been in hopes that if she never spoke of the encounter, it would never be relevant. But also, she had been ashamed of her own conduct in picking a fight.

Not the rich woman, she prayed silently. *One baby of a different species would be bad enough to put in the care of a person like her. But two . . . it doesn't bear imagining.*

"It doesn't say," Henry said, skimming over the article. "It does mention Virgil and Violet at the bottom, not that it calls them by name . . ."

"Let me see," Rose said, flipping the rather-too-cooked egg off the pan onto a plate and pushing the pan away from the burner. She flipped the burner off and grabbed the newspaper away from Henry.

"Ah —" Henry cried, alarmed. "Don't —!"

"'Henry Wainscott, student of paleontology, and his wife, Mrs. Henry Wainscott'?" Rose shouted, reading the bottom paragraph. "Now they can't even be bothered to write my *name?*"

"See, I knew you'd get upset," Henry sighed, rubbing his forehead.

"I've a good mind to call them a third time to set them straight," Rose fumed.

"What good would that do?" Henry asked wearily. "If they didn't listen the first and second time, it's very unlikely they will listen a third."

Rose slammed the newspaper on the table, answering with eloquent silence.

A silver bucket spun into the room at rapid speed, a small green tail whipping around and around outside the edge of it.

Wheeeeeeee! Virgil was having fun!

The bucket slammed against the wall under the window. After a moment, their four-month-old son crawled out, tail first, emanating memories of fun and great dizziness. He wanted to do it again!

"Yes," Rose said, scooping up the bucket, "but since you're in here, you can eat breakfast first. Eggs, ham, or chicken?"

She held her breath, but she shouldn't have.

Chicken! Virgil wanted chicken! Eggs were boring, and ham was yucky yucky yucky!

Rose sighed and opened the icebox door to retrieve the leftover chicken scraps from the previous night. Try as she might to interest Virgil in a cheaper meat, it seemed that poultry was all that was acceptable to him. Not that she had tried that hard, to be fair. Much as she hoped that it was merely pickiness that he would outgrow, she was afraid that it was an instinctive understanding of what food was healthy for him.

With no way to find out save for experimentation, she was too afraid to press the issue and potentially make their son sick. They were not yet poverty-stricken, though Henry's shoulders got tense whenever he added up the sums in his finance book, which did not make her confident that they could go on paying for expensive food indefinitely.

Which reminded her . . .

"How are we for our food budget for this week?" Rose asked her husband casually, setting a bowl full of chicken on the floor and hoping that he would let slip some hint about their budget's general state. It was an intense irritation that he would not share the details of their finances with her.

"Whether we're doing well or not, we have to get another chicken today," Henry said shortly, flipping the paper open. He looked irritable.

Rose was feeling rather indignant herself. His high-handedness about their finances was driving her crazy.

She had finally tried to peek into his finance book the week before last when he had accidentally left it at home while he was at class, surrendering at last to temptation, but she had found nothing but numerous doodles and sketches on most of the pages. What pages there were of sums were unlabeled and clearly unfinished, which made it clear that this was not his finance book, merely another one that looked similar.

Rose had sighed and put it back into his sock drawer, disappointed. If the man would at least explain why he had this mystifying obsession with keeping their finances secret, it would be one thing, but his sullen silence whenever she brought up the subject was maddening.

Virgil brought his head down and smashed it into the side of the metal bowl, horns first. He butted it again, and the bowl toppled over, spilling chicken across the floor. Virgil snarled and dove at the chicken, sending shreds flying all over the room.

"Virgil!" Rose shouted.

Virgil was hunting! Virgil was killing his prey! Rawr! Rawr! It was dying! It was yummy! Yum yum yum yum!

"Just because you are a predatory species doesn't mean you are allowed to have poor manners!" Rose informed him, picking up the scraps of chicken and dumping them back in the bowl, then setting it upright again. "That is not acceptable behavior! Eat properly!"

"He's only four months old," Henry said, snapping the paper slightly as his eyes moved to a top article. "What do you expect him to do, perform with perfect table manners?"

"Given that he can understand everything I say, yes, I do," Rose snapped, picking up a fork to take a bite of her now-cold and overcooked eggs. "He may be exempt from silverware, given that he has no opposable digits, but he mostly certainly can learn some decorum."

"He's not even a toddler," Henry said. "Let the boy eat how he wants to."

Virgil would pretend these were entrails! Yummy yummy!

Rose flinched as a gory scene from one of his ancestors' hunting memories filled her mind. While aware that his was a predatory species, there were certain things that one should not share while others were eating.

Granted, her initial disgust had been immediately replaced by a fascination with how *Tenontosaurus* had been arranged internally, but most people would not be so conciliated by that. And their son did, in fact, need to learn how to behave around those who had no fascination with internal dragon anatomy.

"Virgil," Rose said sternly, "what have I told you? Suppose you shared some memory like that while we were eating dinner at your grandparents' house?"

Virgil's grandfather had thought it was funny! Virgil had done that when he was playing with his grandfather last week! Virgil's grandfather had told him he should do that more often!

Rose put a hand to her forehead. Of course her father had done that.

Virgil was done eating. Virgil wanted to have his bucket back. Could Virgil have his bucket and spin around and around and around in it?

Chapter 3: Fault

Rose sighed and stood to fetch Virgil's toy, which had become extremely dented over the past few weeks. She handed it to him, and watched the little dragon pounce inside, then use his tail to push the bucket faster and faster and faster until it zoomed across the floor.

Wham! Straight into the wall in the living room.

Virgil was having fun! Virgil was dizzy. Virgil would do it again!

Rose took a bite of her eggs, staring at the back of the newspaper Henry still held out in front of him. There was nothing interesting on the back page, but the tiny article within the middle had given her enough to ponder for one day.

CHAPTER 4
Food

As it was Tuesday, one of the days when Henry went to classes and Rose stayed home with the baby, she had no prior obligations to impede her from the crucially important journey she wished to make.

"Virgil and I will be walking down to the museum today," Rose informed her husband as he pulled on his socks, a trifle defensively. She was afraid he would tell her she should mind her own business about the new dragon eggs.

"Sure," Henry grunted, poking his finger through a hole in his sock and letting out an exaggerated sigh.

Rose's fingers tensed. If that were meant to be some sort of hint that she should darn them, she would not oblige him. She did not ask him to mend her stockings, nor had she requested the money to buy more, even though all of the pairs she had remaining looked a dreadful shambles. Having an infant whose species name meant "terrible claw" tended to do that to one's legwear.

But Henry said nothing. He merely pulled on his shoes, which were looking quite worn, and stood.

"I hope you and Virgil have a good time," he said. "Perhaps he'll meet some new friends."

A tiny head poked out of a dented bucket.

Who were Virgil's friends? Who were Virgil's friends he was going to see today?

"Two new dragons," Henry said. "They woke up and they're going to hatch soon. Like you did."

Virgil didn't want to hatch again. Virgil hadn't liked hatching. It had been very uncomfortable, and his parents hadn't helped him at all. Virgil was still mad about that. Virgil's father had said he was going to see friends. Violet was Virgil's friend. Could Virgil see Violet today?

"Perhaps," Rose said. "We'll be in the same vicinity. But first we must acquaint ourselves with the new dragon eggs."

And see to it that neither of them is beleaguered by that atrocious woman, she added silently.

Virgil didn't understand what pets were. Why was Virgil's mother angry that somebody had told his mother he was a pet? Who was that woman? Could Virgil see?

Rose flinched. She hadn't meant for Virgil to catch that wisp of memory. She had, in fact, intended him to not be aware of any of the events of that day. But Virgil was extremely curious, and placed no importance on what his parents wished to share and what they had wished to conceal.

It was rather frustrating. Rose had always assumed that when she moved out of her parents' house, she would no longer be forced to endure the whims of her intrusive younger sisters and their flagrant disrespect for privacy. But after a brief sojourn with two roommates she had not been close with, she was now living with a child who put her younger sisters' snooping prowess to shame.

Virgil didn't know what that meant. Was snooping something to eat? Virgil didn't want it. Virgil's mother kept trying to make him eat food that was yucky yucky yucky. Virgil wanted chicken. Maybe Virgil was hungry now. Could Virgil have more chicken?

"Oh, that reminds me. Could you get more chicken while you're out?" Henry asked, reaching into his pocket to get out his wallet. He pulled out two one dollar bills and handed them to Rose. "Have to visit the bank again soon . . ."

"I could run that errand as well if you add me to the account," Rose said.

"No," Henry said shortly, shutting his wallet with a snap.

Virgil didn't understand what money was. Virgil was hungry. Where was Virgil's chicken? Virgil wanted to disembowel it.

"Goodbye," Henry said, giving Rose a kiss. "I'll see you when I get back, unless you'll be back later than me."

"I likely will be. Have a good time at school."

"That's unlikely," Henry said, "but I'll bear it. Virgil, behave for your mother, will you?"

Virgil always behaved. Virgil behaved like he wanted to!

"Behave the way *she* wants you to," Henry said.

Virgil's mother wanted him to eat yucky food. Yucky yucky yucky. He wouldn't eat it. Could he have his bucket and eat chicken in it?

"Goodbye, then," Rose said, giving Henry a kiss. "I'll see you later this afternoon."

Henry stooped to kiss the tiny dragon on the head, and Virgil butted his head against Henry's hand in a similar show of affection. Then the man left, locking the front door behind him.

Rose watched with a slight smile on her face. Maddening as he could sometimes be, she had quite grown to love Henry. She was glad that Virgil had come into their lives and assembled their family.

Virgil was hungry! Virgil wanted to kill food and eat it! Virgil wanted to kill chicken! Yummy yummy yummy!

Rose snapped out of her reverie and let out a long sigh. *Even if our son feels the need to share his ancestors' gory memories.*

In preparation for leaving, Rose changed Virgil's diaper, washed the breakfast dishes, clothed herself for the day, discovered Virgil's diaper was sagging and atrociously-odored, rediapered the child, scrubbed both diapers clean, discovered that his new diaper was sopping, changed him again, and finally got out the pram to go walking.

Virgil wanted to ride in the bucket! Could Virgil ride in the bucket?

"No," Rose said. "You're riding in the pram."

Virgil wanted to play with the bucket *in* his pram.

"I don't think so," Rose said.

Virgil wanted his bucket! Virgil wanted to ram it against the sides!

"Definitely no bucket," Rose said firmly. "I don't want you breaking the pram."

Virgil wanted his bucket! Virgil wanted it!

Rose picked up the the dragon, walked over to the bathroom, placed him in the bathtub, and plugged her ears. The baby let out an unearthly howl and launched himself against the slippery slides in claw-filled fury. Fire spurted everywhere.

"When you calm down, you can get out," Rose said.

Virgil let out an ear-splitting shriek.

"When you calm down, you can get out," Rose said.

Virgil screamed again.

"When you calm down, you can get out," Rose said.

A loud, thumping noise came from above them. The woman in the apartment above them was not happy with the blood-curdling volume.

I know, Rose thought. *I'm sorry. But there's not much we can do but discipline him and hope he learns to stop screaming.*

Virgil was noticing the ceiling. The ceiling made noise. The ceiling was angry. Why was the ceiling angry?

Rose sighed.

Virgil wanted to get out of the box now. Virgil was calm.

"So you are," Rose said, and leaned over to pick him up. Maddeningly, the dragon's diaper was wet *again*.

She changed him quickly, not worrying much about the pins, since her son's scales were tough enough to be at little risk of harm even if she was careless. Then she placed the dragon in the pram, feeling impatient to get going.

Virgil poked his head out eagerly. This would be fun! Virgil liked going walking! Virgil was going to see Violet!

Rose draped a blanket over the pram to conceal him and keep him warm, opened the door, and took them outside. The air was chilly, so she shivered under her coat as she maneuvered the pram down the stairs. Virgil let out an excited commentary from beneath the blanket, no doubt drawing the image of their surroundings from her mind as she stepped outdoors.

It was very white, and he liked white, because it was fluffy! He had played with lots of snow at Christmas. Could he play with more snow? He wanted to play out in the snow.

"No," Rose said. "We can't afford to buy an extra chicken just because you want to romp. You burn far too much energy keeping yourself warm. Please keep down under the blanket."

Virgil wanted to play. Virgil liked to play. Could Virgil play with Violet? Could Virgil play with Violet right now? He would hit her with his tail, and then she would hit him with her tail, and he would bite it!

"Please don't bite it," Rose said with exasperation. "You made Violet cry last time you bit her tail. Remember?"

Virgil didn't remember. Oh, Virgil remembered because his mother remembered. She was showing him what he'd done. Virgil felt very sad. He hadn't meant to make Violet sad. Virgil was very sad! He was going to cry!

"It's all right!" Rose said quickly, wrenching her thoughts back to better things. The last thing anybody needed was a screaming dragon throwing a fit on the sidewalk. "It's all right. Violet is fine now. See?" She focused her mind on how much happier Violet had been after the pain had subsided.

Virgil felt very sad! Virgil felt better. Virgil wanted his bucket. Could he have his bucket now? He had behaved.

CHAPTER 5
Flood

Nearing the museum, Rose was less than enthusiastic to find a huge crowd surrounding the entrance, elbowing one another to get to the doors through the gigantic crush of humanity.

I should have known, she thought, chagrined. *Why didn't I anticipate this?*

She considered turning around and walking back home, but giving up after coming all this way seemed intolerable. She might take Virgil to see Violet until the crowd died down some, but Central Park Zoo was no doubt also flooded with people wanting to see dragons.

From within the pram, disguised by a thick blanket Rose had draped over the top to both conceal her son and keep him warm in the chilly air, Virgil made his opinion known.

He wanted to see Violet. Could Virgil see Violet? He would claw at her tail and bite her tail.

Rose drew in her breath and looked to the heavens for patience. Then she said, in a low voice in the hopes that the surging crowd ten feet from them would not overhear, "No biting tails. No biting any part of Violet. Now, I want to introduce you to two more baby dragons. Can you behave and not make noise and not communicate to anybody until we're there?"

Virgil wanted to play! Virgil would hit the other baby dragons with his tail!

"Yes," Rose said dryly, "I'm sure you'd like to. But they're currently still in eggs."

Virgil didn't know what that meant. Oh, Virgil's mother knew what that meant. No! Virgil didn't want to go back to the egg! It was dark and boring and squished squished squished!

"No," Rose said in frustration, "I don't mean you. I mean the other two —"

She stopped, appalled to notice that they had spectators. Three children and two adults had paused in their excursion towards the museum. Two of the children's mouths were open, while their parents' eyes were riveted on the pram.

Oh, dear, Rose thought with a sigh. *Virgil's method of communication does tend to attract attention.*

Under normal circumstances, she would studiously ignore confused or curious looks and continue in an unrelenting pace towards her destination. This usually worked to keep unwanted onlookers from approaching after recognizing the oddity of Virgil's commentary. She did not know whether they figured out in retrospect that it had been a telepathic dragon or whether they assumed that they had heard it, as she never stopped to check, but as long as it worked to secure her privacy in the vast majority of situations, she didn't much care.

Unfortunately, that seemed unlikely to work here. For one thing, they had likely been standing there long enough to draw the correct conclusion. And for another, even if they hadn't been, their proximity to the museum suggested that they had come specifically to witness the new telepathic dragons, which would mean the inference would be obvious.

Rose pursed her lips, deciding what to do.

"Hey," one of the children said, "isn't that —"

Rose made her decision. Before the sentence went any further and it would be rude not to answer, she pushed her pram forward to join the frantic crowd. She had meant to enter the museum, and she would do so.

Chapter 5: Flood

Virgil continued to make occasional comments about the crowd, mostly asking Rose the meaning of various glimpses of memories that he had no business plucking from strangers' heads. She shoved the pram through the entrance, at last reaching the doors, and focused very sternly on a memory of telling him just last week not to do that.

Virgil's mother was mean! Virgil was angry! Virgil was going to howl!

No! Rose thought. *No howling! If you want your bucket back, you're not going to howl!*

Virgil settled down. He was behaving. Could he have his bucket?

"When we get home," Rose muttered under her breath.

Virgil was angry! His mother had said he could have his bucket! He was going to howl!

An earsplitting wail rose up from the pram, and heads turned to stare at them from all over the crowd. Rose gritted her teeth and clenched the handle of the pram in frustration.

Since Virgil's unearthly screech more closely resembled a bird of prey than a human child, there would shortly be no concealing what he was to all around them. Rose decided to use the situation to her advantage.

She wrenched off the blanket to put her son on full display. Gasps rang around them, and Rose didn't stop. She scooped up Virgil in one arm and turned to a man near her who appeared to have muscular forearms.

"I need to get to the fourth floor immediately," she said in a no-nonsense tone, waiting until Virgil had paused to breathe. Thankfully, that seemed to act as a distraction for the dragon, who did not recommence screaming. "Would you please carry the pram?"

"Certainly," the man said readily, his eyes focused on Virgil.

The crowd parted to make way for them as they headed up the stairs, all eyes fastened on Virgil as the initial shocked silence moved into a flurry of whispers. Despite the irritation of being a spectacle, Rose felt some gratification that Virgil's tantrum had for once been useful.

They reached the top of the stairs, and the man heaved the pram down to the floor for her.

Rose nodded. "Thank you."

"You're welcome." The man stared at the small dragon in her arms. "Is he —"

"Yes," Rose said, feeling that it was better to get questions over with. "He's the first dragon who hatched from this museum. His name is Virgil. You can find the second one in Central Park Zoo. Her name is Violet."

Virgil liked Violet! He wanted to play with her!

"Can I touch him?" the man asked wide-eyed, reaching out his hand.

Rose sighed internally, but as the man had helped her, it seemed churlish to refuse.

"Yes," she said, "but please make it brief."

A surge of people dove forward, their hands outstretched. Virgil wriggled and started to protest his discomfort as dozens of people shoved their hands all over him.

"Enough!" Rose barked, swatting the uninvited hands away, her patience now at an end. "There may be some parents who don't mind their children being manhandled, but I am not one of them! Please stand back and do not make my son uncomfortable."

The crowd drew back, looking abashed, as the one man gently stroked Virgil's side with a look of awe on his face.

Rose smiled slightly, remembering the first time she had had that opportunity. It was remarkable to realize that one was touching an infant from a species that had gone extinct millions of years ago. It felt miraculous; in fact, it was still unexplained and unfathomable how they had survived so long. She knew that it had happened, yet it still felt impossible.

Taking her leave as soon as it felt polite to do so, Rose deposited Virgil in his pram and draped the blanket over the top again, even though she was not sure if that would accomplish any of the concealment it had before. It seemed prudent to at least attempt to be discreet. Then she headed with great dignity into the Hall of Saurischian Dragons.

The flood of people here was greater that it had been elsewhere, and her attempt at discretion proved extremely useless as the people from the stairs all followed her in, many of them shouting in extreme excitement and pointing at her and her pram.

Attempting to ignore the hubbub that was turning into pandemonium around her, Rose reached the dragon eggs exhibit and then stopped, staring blankly.

There were now only eight eggs on display. Presumably the two who had awakened were the missing ones.

Where did they go? she thought numbly.

CHAPTER 6
Feelings

Yes, of course we moved them," Director Campbell said impatiently in response to Rose's query. "Did you think we'd allow the entire crowd to have access to them?"

Rose had run straight to a museum worker and asked to see the director, and since she had had Virgil with her, she'd been taken to the director's office right away.

Rose nodded slowly. It was obvious; she should have realized that the people here would not be foolish enough to expect that crowds would not flood the museum, and of course the telepathic babies might be very disturbed by the presence of thousands of strange minds pestering them.

"The last thing we need is one of those things bonding to somebody uncooperative," Director Campbell said sourly.

Rose's eyes widened. *That's what he meant?*

The thought of Henry flashed across her mind. He had not been receptive to the museum's original desires to keep Virgil from them, and had in fact been very rude at the director's insistence that the dragon egg belonged to the museum, not to his chosen parents. This had been a fiasco that had only been settled when Virgil had thrown a fit, which the director had not been prepared to handle. It seemed Director Campbell was determined that there would be no more Henrys.

Chapter 6: Feelings

Rose swallowed. She could see things from his perspective, yet — yet fathers like Henry were exactly what it would take to make the infant dragons grow up healthy, well-adjusted, and recognized as people with the same rights as the human majority. While there was no doubt that Harrison Jones loved Violet, he had accepted their circumstances far too amiably.

Which was, perhaps, a type of wisdom. But it would not lead to the future that Rose wished to see for *Deinonychus antirrhopus*. Their species deserved better.

Her son deserved better.

He was lucky he'd gotten it.

Director Campbell could not be allowed to deprive all the future dragons in his museum of parents like Henry.

But Rose knew that openly opposing him could only end in catastrophe. So she swallowed her feelings, and said, "Would I be allowed to visit the awakened dragon eggs? I was thinking that Virgil would like to meet them."

Director Campbell drummed his fingers on his desk, thinking.

Oh, please, Rose thought. *If nothing else, at least let Virgil meet the others of his species.*

"All right," the director said at last. "Teedle is taking care of them. Has them in his office now. As long as you are strictly supervised, you may take that dragon to meet them."

Rose's heart lifted in relief.

"As long as you don't cause any trouble," the director added, frowning. "And I don't want your husband going near them."

Rose's fingers clenched, but she nodded.

Mr. Teedle, the curator of the dragon collection, was a kind man who was close to Rose's father's age. Rose did not have many people she would consider friends, but Mr. Teedle qualified, despite their difference in age. They had known each other since her early years in high school, when she had commenced spending all her spare time in the museum's Research Library.

Mr. Teedle had always been supportive of Rose's plans to become a paleontologist, and he had also been present at Virgil's hatching. So it was no surprise that, when she knocked on the door to his office and he opened it, he greeted her with great warmth.

"Miss Palmer!" he cried, and then quickly corrected himself. "Mrs. Wainscott. I'm pleased to see you! Have you brought Virgil here?"

"I have," Rose said, glancing peevishly at the pram. "And he seems to have decided it was naptime as I was walking here."

"Children are like that," Mr. Teedle chuckled. "They only want to sleep when it's inconvenient."

"I've gained permission to meet the new dragon eggs," Rose said. "Would now be an acceptable time to do so?"

"Of course," Mr. Teedle said, opening the door wide and stepping back.

Heart thumping in excitement, Rose stepped into the room, pushing the pram before her. It was hard to fit the rather large pram into the small room, but Mr. Teedle took charge of correcting that deficiency by moving a chair out of the way. Her gaze fell on the two eggs on the man's desk, still and silent, the same brown-spotted orange shells as the one Virgil had been in.

"Are they . . . awake?" Rose said. She had been about to say *alive*, but that would be a silly question. All the eggs were alive. That was why they weren't fossilized.

"This one is soundly sleeping," Mr. Teedle said, tapping the desk beside the one to the right. "I think perhaps she was awakened before she was ready. This one is napping, but he doesn't usually sleep for long, so you will probably be able to converse with him soon." He tapped a spot on the desk beside the left egg. "I'm afraid he woke the other egg by vigorous telepathic yelling. It was similar to what Virgil did when he was separated from you and Mr. Wainscott, but even more painful and unbearable. I pity his parents, because he seems likely to be a real handful."

Parents, Rose thought, reassured that Mr. Teedle had used the word. It seemed that, no matter what the museum director was planning, the dragon curator took it as a given that the eggs would be raised by proper adults who adopted them.

"Why was he yelling?" she asked politely.

Mr. Teedle frowned. "The same reason as Virgil did, I'm sorry to say. And this time, there is no easy solution."

"What do you mean?" Rose began —

He was a dragon inside an egg. His parents went out hunting. They always had memories to share when they came back, and he couldn't wait to hunt with them. But they had been a long time. A long time. A long time. Where were his parents?!

Minds came and said his parents were gone. Wrong! Wrong! *WRONG!*

They were coming back! They were coming back! They'd said they'd be back, and they were coming back! He was going to scream until they came back for him!

Rose staggered backwards as a silent tidal wave of fury blasted her mind. It was wordless, potent, and vigorous.

"Can you —" Rose gulped, barely able to form the words. "Can you stop, please?"

This was a new mind. Was this mind going to get his parents for him? If this new mind got his parents for him, he would stop screaming.

"I'd love to help," Rose said, "but —"

The blast of fury poured through her mind again. Rose took an involuntary step backwards, then fumbled for the doorknob, desperate to get out of range.

Stop it! Virgil wanted it to stop! Virgil was really mad! Virgil was woken up from his nap!

Rose's gaze flew to the pram, where her son was wriggling around under the blanket. She whipped the blanket back, and Virgil sat there, emanating indignation.

A little uncertainty came from the egg. He was angry. If he screamed enough, his parents would come back. His parents were coming —

Virgil's parents hadn't come back! Virgil had waited for his parents for a long, long time, too! Virgil had found new parents with minds just like his old ones!

No! He was really angry! He didn't want new parents! He was going to scr—

Virgil would share Violet's memories with the angry, mean, annoying person!

Extinction shattered across Rose's mind. Memories from adult dragons who were suffering, starving, bleeding, dying. Everyone was gone now. Even all the eggs were mostly asleep. What had happened? Where was the world? There were no parents left. They were all gone.

EVERYTHING WAS ALL GONE, AND ONLY DESPAIR WAS LEFT.

Rose gasped, shaken. That memory of Violet's was new. It was worse than all the other ones that Violet had shared. It also had a strange, surreal quality that the rest of her memories didn't. Where had it come from? Had it been one of her dreams?

There was dead silence for a minute, and Rose gripped the handle of the pram. She hoped that her son had not traumatized the other infant.

When the answering thought came back, it seemed weak and scared.

He was . . . angry. He was . . .

CHAPTER 7
First

Virgil would share his memories of meeting his new parents now. Then the new mind would see.

New memories filled Rose's head, and these were even stranger than the surreal quality of Violet's dream, because they were familiar, and yet alien. She had been there to experience the whole thing; she had even seen it from Virgil's perspective on that same day. Yet now, they had been painted over with the certainty of hindsight and the optimism of romanticism, implying that this had somehow been fate or destiny.

The new dragon seemed to gobble it up with the hunger of a starving creature. His vicious anger abated, and he started to release impressions that were increasingly hopeful.

This might not be a realistic expectation Virgil is passing on, Rose thought, troubled. *The chances of this new dragon finding two people exactly like his original parents are not high. And even if he does, what are the chances that they won't be married to two other people? Just because Virgil was the first doesn't mean his experience will be representative.*

The angry dragon egg now seemed soothed. Where could he find his new parents? The new ones who would be just like his old ones?

Mr. Teedle cleared his throat. "About that —"

Rage blasted from the dragon egg before the curator could finish his sentence.

No! He wanted his new parents *now!*

"I'm sorry," Mr. Teedle said. "I'm afraid your wants are not the only relevant factor here. They will, of course, be weighed, but there are other things that must be —"

He wanted his parents, he wanted his parents! He wanted his parents, he wanted his parents! He was going to scream! He was going to scream!

Pent-up fury was building to an explosive climax again.

"Perhaps it would be better for you to leave," Mr. Teedle said.

"Can't I meet the other dragon egg first?" Rose asked regretfully.

Mr. Teedle opened his mouth to reply . . .

She was unhappy. She was sleepy. He was noisy. He was disturbing her. She wanted to sleep. She would go back to sleep. He was being noisy.

The feather touch of those impressions faded as quickly as they had come.

Mr. Teedle smiled wryly. "There you have it. That's all we've gotten from her, either."

Rose's mind raced. *Is this another female that my son could eventually court? Do they have compatible personalities?* It was hard to judge from just a few fleeting impressions, but she hoped they might be. The more choices Virgil had, the better his chances of gaining a mate that would please him.

"I'm relieved that there are as many females as males thus far," Rose commented. "If there had been double the number of males, it would have been a problem."

Mr. Teedle nodded. "There still might be. We have no way of knowing what genders the sleeping eggs are, after all. But we can hope for either more females or exact gender equality."

If Rose's child had been a daughter rather than a son, she would have bristled at the hope of extra females. All signs from Virgil and Violet's memories indicated that their species paired monogamously for life, thus too many extra females would put each one at a disadvantage for eventually breeding.

But even under those circumstances, she would have understood that slightly more females would be more of an advantage to an underpopulated species than slightly more males. From a purely cold, biological standpoint, one male could produce offspring with two females simultaneously, while one female could not do the same with two males. While exact gender equality would be preferable for a monogamous species, slightly more females would still be viable.

Of course, *Deinonychus* dragons were people, not livestock. They would make their own choices, and those choices would not always be best for the species. Still, Rose hoped that the initial conditions would at least be optimal for continuance. It was a miracle that *Deinonychus antirrhopus* was still alive today, and she did not want them to die out again from having too few individuals to support a stable population.

Besides, from a selfish perspective, her child was a son. For *him* to have the best chance of eventually producing offspring, extra females would be optimal.

Rose smiled to herself at the thought of how Henry would react if she said any of this to him. He would, no doubt, be indignant that she was even considering their son's future marriage prospects at such a young age. But, after all, her mother's grandparents had been intended for one another from the cradle, and that only because of social snobbery, not biological practicality. She failed to see how this was any different.

As long as I am treating him exactly as I would a human infant, Rose thought, *I am treating him properly.*

All this flashed across her mind exactly as another burst of fury rose up from the left egg.

He was angry! He was angry! He wanted his parents, his parents, his parents! He was going to screeeeeeeeeam!

Rose flinched and staggered backward.

Virgil was mad, too! Virgil was very mad! The mean mind wasn't going to help the other baby find his parents! He was going to screeeeeeeeeam!

"Oh, no!" Rose burst out. "Please don't —"

Two telepathic screams burst out and mingled with the hideously loud one from Virgil's mouth.

Rose seized the opportunity to grab the doorknob as soon as her son stopped to take a breath, then made a rapid exit from the room. She glanced back through the closing door with a mixture of apology and humiliation, and Mr. Teedle merely jerked his head in a nod, looking rather wild-eyed. The door swung shut.

Rose ran down the hallway, the pram bouncing before her, and both the urgency of her mind and the movement seemed to distract Virgil. Away from the instigator, he quieted quickly.

Could Virgil play with Violet now? Virgil liked Violet better. Violet was more interesting. She could roll around and play.

Rose ceased moving, stopping to bury her face in her hands. She had had enough of other people's children for the day, especially draconic ones. Her patience was completely shot, her nerves were frazzled, and she wasn't even sure where she would find the emotional resources to deal with Virgil's constant pestering, pestering, pestering all day.

"Why," Rose murmured, removing her face from her hands and glaring at Virgil, "why must you be even more difficult than a human infant would be?"

Virgil stared at his mother. Virgil didn't understand. Could Virgil play with Violet now? Violet was more interesting.

Rose breathed in deeply, trying to calm her shredded nerves. She was upset on behalf of the new dragon, disappointed that the introduction hadn't gone as well as she'd expected, frustrated with Virgil for making the situation much worse, embarrassed at the stress he had caused Mr. Teedle, and worried that Director Campbell would now treat her like a troublemaker as much as Henry.

How? Rose wondered, smacking her hand on the handle of the pram in fury. *How am I supposed to deal with anything when Virgil keeps making himself such a pest?*

A terrible wave of misery rushed up from the pram. Virgil's mother was sad! Virgil's mother was sad because of him! Virgil had made his mother sad! He was going to cry!

A thin wail rose from the pram, increasing in volume.

"No!" Rose said hastily, moving to draw the blanket back from its curtain concealing her son. "No, Virgil! It's all right. See? I'm fine. Look! I'm fine!"

A fancily-dressed man walked by, bowler hat in hand, and stopped with his mouth gaping open as he saw the individual in the pram.

Not again, Rose thought, tugging the blanket back around the front. She gave a look that dared him to come any nearer. Taking the hint, the man hurried on, though not without a dozen backward glances before he reached the end of the hallway.

Virgil felt better now. Virgil still wanted to play. Could Virgil play? Virgil still wanted to . . .

"All right, all right!" Rose burst out. "You can play with Violet! Just stop pestering me!"

Virgil was happy! Virgil was excited! Virgil would shred this blanket and pretend it was prey!

A terrible ripping sound came from the front of the pram.

"No!" Rose screamed, diving to save it.

Chapter 8
Friends

Inside the zoo, the crowds were nearly as crazy as they had been at the museum. Rose should, perhaps, have expected this.

"Mommy, I wanna see the dragon!" a small child was shouting, dragging a frazzled-looking woman forward as she attempted to juggle a toddler and a purse without letting the toddler grab things out of the opening of the purse.

I know the feeling, Rose thought dryly, and then realized that she didn't. She only had one child, not two, fraying her nerves constantly. The thought of two was terrifying. She amended silently, *I'm glad that I don't know the feeling.*

It took a while to find a zookeeper among the crowd squeezing around Violet's cage, no doubt enjoying another of her ancestors' memories rather than communicating with her as a person. When at last she did make contact, the zookeeper was stressed and less than happy to help, but he did take Virgil, unlock Violet's cage, and place Virgil in with her. Rose managed to squeeze close enough to the front to watch them and be in range of their communication, hoping that this time her son would behave and not be violent in his rambunctiousness.

Hello, Violet! Virgil was saying hello to Violet!

Violet was saying hello to Virgil, too!

Virgil wanted to play! Could Virgil play?

No, Violet was busy.

Bad! Bad! Virgil wanted to play! Virgil would make Violet play!

Virgil charged forward vigorously and snapped at Violet's tail.

Violet let loose a loud shriek, then rolled to the side. She kicked him in the face with one of her back legs as he passed. Her terrible hooked claw caught his nose.

Owwww! Virgil was very unhappy! Violet had hurt him in the snout with her claw!

Rose jerked forward instinctively, despite the fact that she could not reach either of them within the cage, but they had already made up.

Now Violet wanted to play. Violet would play claw catch.

She thrust her leg out, displaying the wickedly hooked claw that gave *Deinonychus antirrhopus* its name, and Virgil dove to catch it. Violet yanked her leg back just in time and smacked him in the face with her tail.

Rose watched with bemusement. The games they invented — or perhaps remembered — were always strange little things. They reminded her more of dogs roughhousing than of any cerebral pastime, yet that wasn't particularly surprising with babies. What did surprise her was how terribly vicious those claws looked, yet how very little they managed to hurt each other.

Now Virgil would play smack-the-claw!

Virgil rolled over onto his back and splayed all four of his legs in the air, kicking them back and forth. Violet rolled over and tried to hit as many of his legs as possible with her own.

They roughhoused back and forth for awhile, until both seemed settled next to each other, curled up on their stomachs, thwacking tails back and forth across each other's backs.

Virgil thought Violet was much more fun than the other baby! That one was in an egg. He was boring.

Violet remembered being in an egg. She hadn't liked it. It had been lonely.

Virgil hadn't been lonely. He had been SQUISHED SQUISHED SQUISHED!

Violet missed her older brother. She missed her parents.

Virgil didn't miss the egg. He had been SQUISHED SQUISHED SQUISHED!

Violet had met lots of parents who wanted eggs. They told her they wanted babies. Sometimes they told her without wanting to tell her. Did the egg want parents?

Virgil didn't remember. Oh, Virgil remembered. Violet was remembering for him.

Rapid impressions flashed through Rose's mind. She realized with a start that there had been memories mixed in with those long bursts of rage. She'd completely missed them because the emotion had been so overpowering, but Virgil had caught them, and now Violet had them.

Violet was disappointed. None of those memories were the same as the parents who came to the zoo wanting eggs.

Well, naturally not, Rose thought. *How common can it be to find two people who have similar minds? It's astounding that Virgil found both me and Henry.*

Violet had an idea. This mind was like that ancestor. Maybe that baby would have this mind as his father.

Rose stared at the dragons intently. As always, they showed no facial expressions, but their tails had stopped flicking, and they seemed to have an air of concentration.

Violet would tell these two they were now that baby's parents. Then those parents would be happy and that baby would be happy and Violet would be happy and then she could play with the baby and she wouldn't be lonely anymore.

Virgil didn't like that baby's parents.

Violet would tell them next time they came. They came a lot. She would tell them she had found their baby. Then their baby could be in the zoo with her, and she wouldn't be lonely.

Virgil didn't like that baby's parents. Virgil had seen one of them in his mother's memories. His mother didn't like that one, so Virgil didn't like her.

Rose sucked in her breath. *Oh, surely NOT . . .*

The argument now took on the tone of a squabble.

Virgil didn't like that baby's parents!

Violet wanted that baby to have those parents! They wanted somebody else to take care of their baby, so that baby could live in the zoo with her! Violet wouldn't be lonely!

Virgil was really mad! Violet wanted a friend other than him! Virgil was going to scream!

The earsplitting shriek burst across the crowd, sending hands flying to cover ears and provoking yells at her loud son to be quiet. That just made Virgil madder, and he screamed even louder and higher-pitched.

Finally, the zookeeper unlocked the cage, hauled Virgil out, and surged through the crowd to deposit the angry little dragon in Rose's arms.

"I think that's it for the day," he said shortly.

Nodding while trying to plug her ears with her shoulders while simultaneously holding on to the source of the squirming, scaly temper tantrum, Rose dumped the angry dragon into the pram, yanked the blanket over the front, and set forth through the crowd. As soon as they were moving, Virgil's scream faded, and he went to sleep.

If he gets that mad about his friend making a new friend, she thought peevishly, *I am definitely glad he does not have any siblings.*

Rose was in a fine temper by the time she got home, especially when she discovered that Virgil's sleeping nostrils had singed a hole in his blanket.

"So somebody else might have a dragon child they choose to put in a zoo," Henry said shortly when she told him the whole situation that afternoon. "What of it?"

Rose stared at her husband in disbelief. She'd thought that he, of all people, would understand how she felt. "For the good of *Deinonychus antirrhopus* —"

"For crying out loud, Rose!" Henry exploded. "Do you think

you can decide how everybody else chooses to raise their children? You may dislike somebody else's choice of parenting, but it's not your decision to make!"

"But for the good of all the other dragons in the future —"

"Maybe you can leave their living arrangements to their own parents, too," he snapped.

Rose flinched, as if struck. She realized that she must have come across as nosy. This chagrined her, because she had spent most of her childhood in a battle with her sisters for privacy. Yet this was not just something that would only affect individuals outside their family.

"I would be willing to," Rose said in a low voice. "But will Director Campbell be willing to?"

Henry said nothing, and she thought she saw a hint of worry flit across his face.

"We can't control that," he said at last. "We can only do what we can do."

But if we don't try, Rose thought, *there are children who will suffer in the future.*

She knew already that she would be going back to the museum tomorrow. She would go early, before her classes. It would be Henry's day to watch Virgil, so she could go alone. Perhaps that would go better than bringing the infant with her.

Someone had to speak up.

CHAPTER 9
Fortitude

Her first class started at eleven, so Rose stood at the entrance to the American Museum of Natural History at ten o'clock, waiting for the doors to open. She would have only half an hour to speak her mind before she had to leave to walk to her first class at Hunter College. She prayed that that would be enough, and that the consequences would not be disastrous.

But consequences or not, she had to speak. There were times when one could not afford to stay silent.

As soon as the doors opened, Rose hurried through the doors, removing her hat and coat and scarf and draping them over her arm as she took the stairs at a rapid pace. The building was far less crowded than it had been yesterday, a welcome change, though she suspected that this was only due to the time of day. Most likely it would be a surge of humanity again later.

Despite the desperate hurry, Rose dawdled for a few minutes inside the Hall of Ornithischian Dragons, watching the *Triceratops* and *Stegosaurus* skeletons, so different from her son and yet so eerily similar. The wings of the *Triceratops* rose high in the air, while the wings of the *Stegosaurus* were spread wide, only a few feet out of reach of prodding fingers, as if it were about to lift off the ground at any moment.

What would it have been like if our son had been a herbivore? Rose wondered. *Would he have been easier to care for?*

It was a ridiculous question, of course, because species such as *Triceratops* and *Stegosaurus* had not had large enough brains to be intelligent. Still, if Virgil had been herbivorous, or even omnivorous such as *Ornithomimus velox*, life might have been much simpler.

Rose shook herself, reminding herself sternly that her role was not to wish that her son had been different, and she was in a hurry besides. She tore herself away from the remarkable skeletons and headed towards her destination, the director's office, a course which she really should not have deviated from in the first place.

But as she stood at the door to the office, summoning her fortitude, she heard angry voices rise from inside.

What? Rose thought dumbly. *Am I too late? Is he meeting with somebody? I thought that at this time of morning, he would not be busy, but perhaps that was naive . . .*

"Well, of course he's coming with us!" a woman's voice shouted, loud enough to reverberate through the door. "The dragon in the zoo said that he'd be ours, and he will be!"

Hair rose at the back of Rose's neck. There was no doubt who that voice belonged to.

"You can't just waltz in here and make demands!" the director's voice said angrily. "Who do you think you are?"

"I AM BESSIE!" the woman's voice announced at a great volume.

Rose put a hand to her forehead. The arrogance was astonishing.

There was a murmur of another voice behind the door, and then an irritated grumble. Before Bessie could raise her voice yet again, Rose knocked politely on the door.

"Who is it?" the director's voice shouted.

Rose turned the handle and gingerly opened the door, standing in view.

"Oh," Director Campbell grumbled. "You."

That did not bode well for a future conversation, and Rose felt a little hurt at being included in his irritation. Still, she supposed she could not blame the man, particularly if Mr. Teedle had mentioned Virgil's behavior yesterday.

"Is there anything else you want?" Director Campbell asked sarcastically. "Your own country club, perhaps?"

"No," Rose said, "I only wanted to speak with you about a matter of some importance. That can wait, however. May I make an appointment?"

"Oh, you!" the woman cried, turning to look at Rose.

She, and a man mostly obscured from Rose's view, were standing rather than seated. The formerly-fur-coated woman now wore a dress of navy blue silk Georgette crepe with fine beadwork on the waist, cuffs, and tunic. A fashionable wool cape with knitted pom-poms was thrown back from her shoulders, and she also had not removed her hat, which had a feather perched on top.

It was clearly not the clothing of a woman struggling to make ends meet. Rose wondered whether this was everyday wear, or whether she had dressed more finely than usual, considering this a special occasion.

"I remember you!" the woman continued. "You gave me the idea to adopt Philomel!"

"Philomel?" Rose asked.

"That's what we're going to call him," the woman said grandly.

Without even meeting the child? Rose wondered.

The director's face had gone very unfriendly. "You gave her the idea?" he growled.

"Not by any deliberate design," Rose said emphatically. "We met in the park, and I informed her that her assessment of *Deinonychus* dragons as mere animals was wrongheaded. She conceived the idea of adopting one on her own."

"Yes, and what Bessie wants, Bessie gets," the woman announced, adjusting her cape and tossing her hair.

Rose could not believe such sheer hubris existed. What kind of life had this woman led, to have such audacity?

Then the man, who Rose had nearly forgotten was there, spoke up.

"We would be happy to make a generous donation to the museum, director." His voice was quiet. "We will, of course, also defer to experts for anything the child needs."

Director Campbell's expression went quite sour.

"And who could possibly make better parents than *us*?" Bessie demanded, stretching her arms widely and beaming.

Rose could think of many.

"We have quite a few friends in important places," the man behind Bessie said mildly. "The mayor, for instance. I can speak with him about this situation. He might, as they say, vouch for us."

It was impressive that he had just made a veiled threat without actually making a veiled threat.

Director Campbell did not seem to miss the hidden meaning, either. His eyes narrowed, and he did not look more receptive.

This situation seemed likely to deteriorate, and nobody seemed to be considering the most important factor of all. Rose weighed her options quickly, then decided that if she was going to speak up, now was a good time to do it.

"Why don't we leave it to the dragon?" she asked.

The director and Bessie turned to look at her.

"The dragon?" Bessie asked, as if Rose had made the most absurd suggestion in the world.

"The dragon?" Director Campbell repeated, as if he agreed.

"Yes," Rose said. "You're talking about the future of a child. Why not let the child's input make the final decision?"

Director Campbell frowned, and Rose thought for a moment that he would outright refuse. But then a sneaky smile spread across his face. "If the dragon rejects them, will they give up on all of this?"

"That won't happen," Bessie said haughtily.

The director looked at the quiet man sharply.

"Yes." The man shrugged. "I'd see no value in having a child that didn't want me."

"Good." The director smiled, resembling a crocodile. "Very good. I'm glad to hear that. In that case, let's introduce you two to the egg."

Chapter 9: Fortitude

He pushed the chair back from his desk and stood. He walked out the door, trailing the haughty woman and her silent husband, and Rose followed them both.

She had no idea what the egg might pick, though she hoped it wouldn't be the haughty woman. But either way, a future that the dragon chose for himself would be better than any forced on him.

No matter what that future might be.

$\mathscr{C}$HAPTER 10
Future

Gathering in the Research Library, where the two eggs had apparently been moved, Rose waited nervously for the two eggs to wake up. To her surprise, it was the female one who awakened first.

There were new minds here. Were these minds her parents?

"Yes," Bessie said eagerly. "We're —"

No, these new minds weren't her parents. She would go back to sleep.

Bessie's jaw jutted out, and her eyebrows lowered. She looked very put out.

"That's one down," Director Campbell said gleefully.

"That's all right," the other man said mildly. "She's not the one we were thinking of, anyway."

They waited for awhile, and neither egg stirred.

"Why isn't he awake now?" Bessie fumed. "I don't like being kept waiting!"

If you don't like being inconvenienced, I suggest you not have children, Rose thought, amused.

Before anyone could stop her, Bessie dove forward, seized the egg, and shook it vigorously.

"Hey!" Director Campbell shouted.

"That could be dangerous!" Rose shouted, too.

"Bessie —" her husband began.

But just as Director Campbell reached to snatch the egg, a familiar emotion began to fill the room. An intense emotion. One that Rose remembered all too well from yesterday.

Rage. Rage. Rage. He was angry! He was angry! Someone had shaken him awake!

"Bessie, that was not well done," her husband said.

He was angry! He was angry, he was angry! He was angry, he was angry, he was angry!

"Your name is Philomel," Bessie announced grandly. "And we are Bessie and Francis, your parents."

That was not his name! That was not his name! He was Crimson! His parents had said he would be crimson, so now he was Crimson!

"That is not a name," Bessie said coldly. "That is a color."

He was Crimson, he was Crimson, he was Crimson!

"We were hoping we could be your parents," Francis said. "But you must make the decision. Will you accept us, or will you not?"

Rose drew in her breath. She glanced at Director Campbell, whose smug facial expression was belied by the tenseness of his shoulders.

He was confused. He liked Francis, but not Bessie. Could he have Francis, but not Bessie?

"No," Francis said. "You can have both of us, or neither. We come together."

He didn't like that! He was angry! He was angry, he was angry, he was angry!

"I'm angry, too!" Bessie snapped indignantly. "What do you have against me?"

"Well," Director Campbell said, grinning broadly, "there's no need to trouble your pretty little head about that, is there? Seeing as the egg's made his decision. Now, if you'd be so kind as to . . ."

"*Pretty little head?!*" Bessie roared, spinning on him. "Maybe the papers were right! Maybe this *is* similar to my cause! Maybe I should focus on dragons' rights instead!"

Crimson was thinking about it. Crimson was still angry. Crimson's mother understood how it felt to be angry. Maybe Crimson's mother could be mad with him together.

"No!" Director Campbell shouted.

Crimson wanted to go home with his new parents now. Their memories showed their cave was big and had lots of space. Crimson's old parents had had a big cave with lots of space. Maybe these parents would be just like his old ones.

"No!" Director Campbell shouted.

CRIMSON WAS ABSOLUTELY FURIOUS, AND HE WAS GOING TO MAKE THAT PLAIN!

Rose doubled over as a piercing headache slammed into her. Director Campbell looked ill. The dragon's emotion was potent and powerful.

Neither Bessie nor Francis looked terribly affected.

"Yes, yes, yes, we know you're in a bad mood," Bessie said impatiently. "But could you rein it in? You're going to make it very difficult to find a nanny if you keep behaving like that."

"It should be fine as long as we pay enough," Francis said briskly. "But I agree, he needs to learn to control that temper first thing. If he doesn't, he will be a holy terror when he hatches and his fire comes in. I wonder if breathing exercises will work as well for dragons as for humans?"

"We should ask the nanny about that," Bessie said grandly. "I'm sure it won't be long before he's fit to introduce to society."

Rose gaped at them.

"You must be joking!" Director Campbell expostulated. "The zoo is better equipped to handle any —"

"My dear, sir," Francis said calmly, "how exactly do you think the zoo would deal with a child with this kind of rage? You don't want him out in public. Neither do they. The obvious solution for all concerned is for him to be cared for by two people who are willing to teach him to not be a danger to those around him."

"Or three people," Bessie said, adjusting her feathered hat, which she had still not removed. "Or more. Depending on how many we hire."

Chapter 10: Future

"Believe me," Francis said with a hint of amusement, "it would be a far better use of your time to agree right now. She makes a better ally than enemy."

An ally. Rose glanced over at the woman, who was tossing her head arrogantly. *An ally. She said that she would fight for dragons' rights. Is that what she is?*

She was not an ally that Rose would have chosen. She was not a person that Rose wished to be well-acquainted with. But maybe . . . just maybe . . . she might be what *Deinonychus antirrhopus* needed:

A pigheaded individual who did not accept social niceties or limitations.

The argument raged for another half an hour, and Rose stayed until she realized that she had missed her entire first class. She remonstrated herself fiercely as she fled to reach her second in time.

Still, by then it was already obvious what the conclusion to the argument was going to be.

The third dragon was going to have a home. And it wasn't going to be in the zoo.

If nothing else, she could be very grateful for this.

CHAPTER 11
Family

Pushing open the door to the apartment and pocketing her key, Rose found Henry asleep on the couch and Virgil rolling around in his bucket. Chicken was strewn across the kitchen floor, and Virgil's backside, obvious as the bucket rolled past, was soaked and smelly.

For a moment, annoyance rose in her chest — what was he doing asleep? But then she breathed deeply, reminding herself that she had seen more than enough anger for one day. She was very grateful that Virgil was reasonably pleasant and Henry was kind and thoughtful most days.

So we have bad days sometimes, Rose thought, leaning over to pick up a textbook that had fallen from Henry's hands when he'd fallen asleep. *We're very, very lucky for the rest of our days.*

She paused, taken aback. This wasn't Henry's textbook. This was the blank book covered in sketches and doodles that she had found a few weeks ago, the one she had mistaken for his finance book.

Thoughtfully, Rose sat down and flipped through the pages. She hadn't looked at it for long before, only long enough to be frustrated that it hadn't held the secrets of their financial state, but now she looked at the art to appreciate it for its own sake.

It was really very good.

There were sketches of Virgil, inked portraits of their family together, and skeletons of other dragon species. On some pages were plants, or perspective studies of streets, or doodles of children playing. She saw a few pictures of people she recognized vaguely from their wedding, members of Henry's family.

Why did he hide this? she wondered.

She glanced up, and saw that Henry's eyes had opened and he was watching her.

"I'm sorry," Rose said immediately, snapping the book shut. "I didn't mean to pry. I only — it was lying on the floor, and I picked it up —"

"It's all right," Henry said with a sigh. He sat up and rubbed his eyes. "You'd've found out sometime anyway."

"Found out what?" Rose asked, confused.

"That I'm terrible at sums," he said.

Rose stared at him blankly. Then realization dawned.

"This *is* your finance book?!" she asked incredulously. "But there's barely anything math-related in it!"

"I *told* you I was terrible at sums," he said defensively. "That's why it drives me crazy when you want a running commentary. I don't know where we are half the time. I wish I didn't have to do it in the first place!"

"Well, but . . . But it's . . ." Rose sputtered. "*This* is your finance book?!"

"I know, I know," he muttered, putting his head in his hands. "I can't balance a budget if my life depended on it. Numbers just do not make sense to me. I'm sorry."

Rose stared at him in astonishment, at first unable to speak. Then she burst out laughing.

"What?" he demanded, raising his head. "What's so funny?"

Rose couldn't stop herself from giggling. "Then why didn't you ask me to do the budget? I'm fine with numbers!"

"But — but —" he sputtered. "But I'm supposed to do it!"

Rose couldn't stop laughing. "My mother does all the accounts for my family's household. My father hates doing them. Why did you think that would bother me?"

"Well . . ." Henry rubbed his hand through his hair vigorously. "Well, my father always said . . ."

Rose laughed and got up on the couch beside him. She kissed him and handed him the book. "I'll tell you what. You keep drawing those wonderful pictures, and I'll do the finances."

Relief spread across Henry's face. "Well, if you insist . . ."

The dented bucket went flying across the floor and whammed into the couch. A tiny head poked out of it.

Virgil was dizzy. Virgil was having fun. Virgil's mother was home!

"Hi, Virgil," Rose said, smiling, leaning over to pick him up. She had never realized before just how much she liked him and how usually pleasant it was to be around him. Fit-throwing notwithstanding, and his dreadful habit of screaming, he was usually a happy child who was pretty well-behaved for his age.

A terrible odor emanated from their son's hindquarters.

"I changed the last one," Henry said immediately.

Rose groaned in mock annoyance, but she was in too good a mood to argue. She stood and carried Virgil to the bathroom, where she raided the cache of folded diapers they kept under the sink. The diaper change was every bit as dreadful as she had anticipated, especially since Virgil kept on swinging his tail through it, but it was accomplished at last, and she returned to the living room with a cheerful little dragon who kept telling her that she should climb into his bucket with him, heedless of her explanations that she wouldn't fit.

"You know," Henry said, tapping the book that was now on his lap, "this is the reason we met in the first place."

"It is?" Rose asked, setting Virgil on the floor. Their son immediately dove for his bucket.

"Yes," Henry nodded. "The whole reason I went to the museum that day was to sketch the dragons. I was going through a period where I was fascinated with *Stegosaurus*. I thought I'd get a better perspective on the wings if I went to look at them in person."

"And now?" Rose asked.

"Now I prefer *Deinonychus*."

Rose smiled.

Virgil *loved* his bucket! Virgil was going to play in his bucket! Virgil was going to roll right into a wall! *Wham!* Virgil had rolled into a wall! Virgil loved rolling into a wall! Virgil would roll into another wall! *Wham!*

"You can tell me anything, you know," Rose said, taking her husband's hand. "You don't have to keep secrets from me."

Henry nodded. He patted her hand and stared at their laps for a long moment. Then he looked up, a glint in his eyes.

"Well," he said, "there is *one* I probably ought to keep."

"What?" Rose asked indignantly.

He grinned. "I'm not telling you what I'm getting you for your birthday."

Virgil knew what his father was thinking about! His father was thinking about —

"No!" Henry shouted. "Don't you tell her, either!"

www.ingramcontent.com/pod-product-compliance
Lightning Source LLC
Chambersburg PA
CBHW022121050726
47591CB00002B/886